I MUST TELL JESUS

My Lessons & Memories from Calvary

Bertram Be'Jay Major

Entegrity Choice Publishing
PO Box 453
Powder Springs, GA 30127
info@entegritypublishing.com
www.entegritypublishing.com
770.727.6517

Printed in the United States of America

Library of Congress Cataloging-in-Publication Data
ISBN 979-8-9850792-4-1
Library of Congress Control Number: 2022920162

DEDICATION

Firstly, I dedicate this book to my parents and my grandmother. They constantly support me in everything that I do.

Equally, I want to dedicate this book to Pastor Emeritus Rev. Dr. Clyde Hill, Sr and the entire Mt. Calvary Baptist Church family. I really didn't want to name people individually because I don't want to leave anyone out. When I say the entire Mt. Calvary family, I mean everybody! To the past and present members, this book is dedicated to you.

I will be amiss if I didn't mention Ms. Dora. I dedicate this book to her because she really blessed me by gifting me with past videos of Mt. Calvary. God gave me the go-ahead to write this book, but the videos from Ms. Dora gave me more excitement and joy to write this book. Watching the videos brought back past lessons and memories that I had forgotten.

Lastly and most importantly, I want to dedicate this book to my Lord and Savior Jesus Christ! Without him, none of this would be possible.

CONTENTS

INTRODUCTION

GROWING UP, a hymn that was ministered by my home church pastor almost every Sunday for altar call (intercessory prayer) still ministers to me to this day. *"I Must Tell Jesus,"* is my absolute favorite hymn.

I must tell Jesus all of my trials;
I cannot bear these burdens alone;
In my distress He kindly will help me;
He ever loves and cares for His own.

I must tell Jesus all of my troubles;
He is a kind, compassionate friend;
If I but ask Him, He will deliver,
Make of my troubles quickly an end.

I must tell Jesus!
I must tell Jesus!
I cannot bear my burdens alone;
I must tell Jesus!
I must tell Jesus!
Jesus can help me, Jesus alone.

My relationship with Jesus Christ is special and real. I first heard about this man named Jesus as a child at my home church, "Mt. Calvary Baptist Church." Mt. Calvary is not a perfect church, but it's where I first heard about Jesus. No church is perfect, I just had to point that out. It's amazing the way Mt. Calvary has played a huge part in my life, from the songs sung by the choir to the powerful, Holy Spirit filled messages and lessons from my home church pastor, among other things. My memories and lessons from Mt. Calvary really are unique and life-changing.

I wasn't a normal average kid growing up. Yes, I loved watching cartoons, playing video games, etc. but I was fascinated not just with church but with this man named "Jesus." Every time I went to church, I was always happy to be there and to learn more about Jesus. When it comes to my relationship with Jesus, my prayer is that my story will help you in your walk with Christ. Also, for those who have not accepted Christ, I pray it helps you realize that Jesus lives and Jesus saves.

I knew after my first book was published that I would want to write a book about Mt. Calvary. Well, God has given me the go-ahead to do that right now.

One last thing, don't think less of your memories and lessons in life. Whether it's good or bad, it's a part of your journey. It's up to you to determine how it affects your life. One thing I have found out during my life is that through Jesus, I don't have to settle.

I'm not perfect; I have messed up a lot in life, but through Christ, I've been forgiven. Yes, forgiveness is available, but that does not mean we do wrong on purpose. Learn from your mistakes and struggles in life. Don't let Satan or anyone make you think you are a lost cause. Your lessons and memories play a huge role in your life. If you don't believe me, keep reading. Come go with me on my journey down memory lane.

CHAPTER 1

MY EARLIEST MEMORIES

AS I'M WRITING THIS BOOK, I have a huge smile on my face. When I think of my earliest memories, I remember one of the deacons singing the song, *"I'm Going to Stay Under the Blood."* That song is one of the songs that have played a part in my relationship with Jesus. I didn't understand the meaning of the song as a kid but I understood it more as I got older. That hymn used to be one of the first hymns I heard on a Sunday morning worship service. After a few hymns and prayers, I remember seeing my pastor coming in with the other associate ministers. Being a child at the time, I always had this exciting feeling at the start of Sunday service. I was excited to see what song was going to be sang, what prayer was going to be prayed, what laugh was going to be laughed, what Word was going to be preached, and who was going to come Christ at the end. It's interesting thinking back on this because I now noticed how much I was being touched by the Lord at a young age.

By the time my pastor and the associate ministers made it to the pulpit, either my pastor or one of the other ministers would do the call to worship. Then I used to look over in the corner where the musicians were, and I can remember hearing the hymn *"Sweet Holy Spirit"* start to be played. This hymn always set the atmosphere, and the Holy Spirit definitely took over even more. Keep in mind, I was a child, so I was super short. It was a struggle trying to look at and see everything but somehow, I always found a way to see everything. Whether I was picked up by my mom, standing on the tip of my toes, etc. I was going to find a way to see. I'm laughing so hard right now, but I used to be so frustrated at that.

Once the congregation finished singing *"Sweet Holy Spirit,"* it was time for the choir to make their way to the choir stand. Now I really got excited to see the choir come in. Hearing the song *"Glad to Be in the Service"* playing and watching them come in always put a huge smile on my face. You knew for a fact it definitely was service time once you heard the song, *"Glad to Be in the Service."* Between that point of the service and when it was time for the sermon, songs were ministered, the offering was lifted, visitors were welcomed and greeted, announcements were made, and with all of that, God was having His way. Then it would be time for the main course of service, "the Word." My home church pastor would always say, "Before preaching time, it's praying time."

Here's a fact I kind of touched on in the introduction. Not only has the hymn *"I Must Tell Jesus"* taught me about prayer and how Jesus is always there to help, but my pastor always broke down what prayer is, how important it is, and the fact that we all can go to God in prayer ourselves. When it was time for altar call (intercessory prayer), he would read the sick and shut-in list and prayer requests and mention those who were going through the process of grief. In the background, you could hear the song being played. You knew that it was time for us to pray. It wasn't a time to be cute or play around; it was definitely praying time. It was time to not just pray for our own personal life, but it was a time to pray for others. After a few words of preparation, he would ask us all to stand and call us to the altar. Those who desired would make their way to the altar. We would gather at the altar and grab the hand of the person next to us. Then after everyone gathered, my pastor would start singing the hymn *"I Must Tell Jesus."*

There was a lot I had to learn and one of those things was not looking around. I remember being tapped on my shoulder by my mom telling me to look forward and keep my head bowed. The reason I remember doing that is I used to look at how some people were reacting. Not to be nosy, but it's like you felt the heaviness of others. The tears I saw falling and the cries of help that were being cried out to the Lord—it just made it all real for me as a kid. One thing that did scare me as a child is when someone who fall out in the Spirit because I really didn't understand that until I got older. After he sang *"I Must Tell Jesus"* and prayed, we went back to our seats, and it would be time for the Word. Now I can go on and on about my pastor's sermons, but you are going to hear A LOT about his sermons as you read through this book.

Another early memory I have is the time in which we weren't able to make it to church sometimes but tuned into the service on the radio. I remember my great grandfather's black radio by his bed. His church didn't have service every Sunday.

I remember waiting until it was time for service to start. When it was time, he would turn to the station. Either the choir was singing or my pastor was starting the first verse of *"I Must Tell Jesus."* Those were some rememberable times. These are my earliest memories of Mt. Calvary. As a child, I knew my calling, but I had no clue what the road ahead had in store for me. My life was in for a roller coaster of a ride.

CHAPTER 2

CASSETTE TAPES AND VIDEOS

BEFORE I GO ANY FURTHER, I would be wrong if I didn't mention purchasing cassette tapes, videos, CDs, and DVDs from Mt. Calvary. Only because this has been a huge part of my Christian journey over the years, especially during my bouts with depression and suicidal thoughts in my teen years (I'm going to talk about that later in this book). I purchased the worship services from the past and present because of the songs and the Word. Both always gave me what I needed. Now let me tell you a very funny fact. There have been worship services from the past that I didn't purchase the cassette tape or video. Time would pass, and I would either forget the date of the service or when I did remember, the cassette tape was available but the video wasn't. I used to laugh at myself for not getting stuff right away. There were also a few times the cassette tape wasn't available but the video was. Sometimes, I purchased cassette tapes trying to find a sermon my pastor had preached because I could not remember the actual date. In a lot of cases like that, I have been successful (I'm writing that with a smile and laugh). I still have a lot of services on video I need to locate. Hopefully, I will find those one day soon. In the process though, I would be reminded of certain songs, moments, and sermons from those cassette tapes and videos that were right on time. Some stuff I didn't even remember, but it still blessed my soul. I even purchased a service from when I was super young and wasn't old enough to have a memory because I love to hear sermons from back then.

Now I'm in my 30s, and I still purchase CDs and DVDs because staying in the Word is something I strongly believe in. Every Sunday I'm at church, I make sure I get a Word and apply it to my life. To be real, it gets rough throughout the week. Whether it's a message or song on YouTube or a message or song from Mt. Calvary, I'm going to make sure I get what I need to continue my Christian race. I thank God for the audio & visual ministry of the Mt. Calvary Baptist Church. They will never know and understand the role they have played in my life. Even down to my online community ministry which I've had since age eleven, having those recordings has blessed me and kept me focused on Christ. Before I end this chapter, I must mention one of my fellow choir members from Calvary.

During the pandemic, I went through a lot, and she gifted me with A LOT of videos from Mt. Calvary. I always wanted to write this book, but God kept telling me it wasn't time. One day I was watching one of the videos that she gave to me, and I clearly heard God tell me that it was time to write this book. To my fellow choir member (you know who you are), thank you for blessing me with those videos. Watching so many powerful

Holy Spirit filled services and choir anniversaries have really blessed and ministered to me.

As this book continues, in certain chapters, I'm going to mention the worship services and sermons that have meant so much to me. By the way, I wish I had all of them on video. Even though so many years have passed, the Word of God never changes. I pray that as you continue reading, you receive many blessings from the Lord.

Early Experiences with Jesus Christ

In the late 90s, my age was still a single digit. However, I was just a few short years away from turning ten years old. As I got closer to that, I started to have thoughts and experiences. I would be thinking a lot about what can Jesus do for me? What is it like getting saved and having Jesus Christ as Lord and Savior? Not only that, I would have experiences. I would start to feel different in service and start to become more focused on wanting him to move within me. I didn't realize this until my late teens or early 20s, but I was starting to be touched by the Holy Spirit. I knew I had this calling to preach one day, but I was starting to get more and more curious about Jesus. I was going to Sunday school and Bible study, so I was learning as much as I could, but I wanted more!

I want every adult to know this: don't ever ignore when a child is talking about Jesus. That didn't happen to me, but I have seen it happen to a lot of kids over the years. You can't pray for the Holy Spirit to touch someone and then ignore or doubt when it happens. I knew my life was changing and that it was time for me to do something. I knew what needed to happen in order for me to truly experience who Jesus Christ really is. Which brings me to the year 1999, the year I accepted Jesus Christ as my Lord and Savior.

CHAPTER 4

Take Me to the Water

(August 1999)

On sunday, August 22, 1999, at age seven and a half, I accepted the Lord Jesus Christ as my personal Savior. That Tuesday night, I was baptized. Looking back, I knew God had His hand on my life and that he was surely showing me my calling and purpose in life. I wanted to learn more and get to know Jesus more. My parents wanted to make sure I understood what becoming saved really was. I remember telling them that I wanted to be baptized and let Jesus into my heart, but they just wanted to be sure I was ready. To this day, I don't hold anger or frustration toward them about that because it all worked out the way God wanted it to. I wasn't like a normal kid; I did kid things, though. I played video games, watched TV, played outside, and love goofing off. But I always talked about church and Jesus to kids my age and even adults. I got picked on a lot and was oftentimes left out of stuff because of it. I also remember going with my great grandfather to his church sometimes, and he continuously told me to always follow the Lord.

Leading up to accepting Christ into my life, something that had been on my mind, started to be on my mind even more. That something was becoming a preacher, and I knew that it was something very important and serious to me. I remember being told by some people that it would happen one day but I was too young to know what I want or wanted to be. I hate that cliché! You can do anything you put your mind to! However, don't twist my words. I'm not saying do something you absolutely know is wrong or use this as a way to break the law or even worse.

"God is not an author of Confusion, but of
peace, as in all churches of the saints."
I CORINTHIANS 14:33 (KJV)

Don't let nothing stop you from becoming successful or from discovering and fulfilling your God-given purpose. I knew that whatever God has for me, he must become fully a part of my life. To be connected to him, I must first accept Jesus Christ into my life.

In August 1999, I reached a point where I didn't care what anyone said or thought. I approached my pastor and said, "I want to accept Christ into my life as my Savior and be baptized." At the time, I thought that once the doors of the church were open, if I tried to walk to the front, my mom would stop me. This is so funny to me because looking back at this, I thought I was going to get into trouble. I respected my mom and dad, and the last thing I wanted to do was disobey them. I just said to myself, "Jesus, I heard you can do anything. I know what I'm planning to do is right, but this may not make my parents happy, so please protect me if they get mad."

With the fear of being held back, I waited until service was over and everybody was leaving. I was sitting between my mom and my grandmother (my mom's mother). I told both of them that I was going to talk to the pastor and that I would be right back. Now here's the funny part to the story. My grandmother knew what I was up to and, from a distance, she followed me. My mom knew something was up but didn't really know. But that didn't stop her from following. I made it to the pastor. There were a lot of people around him that were talking to him. I remember pulling on his robe (because I was super short) to get his attention. He looked down and said, "Hey, son, how are you?" Instead of saying fine, I said boldly, "Pastor, I want to be baptized." Everyone around us stopped, and my pastor's smile became even bigger. He then grabbed the microphone and looked upstairs to the audio ministry to tell them to turn the microphone on. While that was happening, he asked me what my name was. I looked at him closer and said, "My whole name?" He replied, "Yes, son." I told him my whole name and once the microphone was turned on, he said, "My brothers and sisters, this young man (he then said my full name) has decided that he wants to accept Jesus Christ into his life and wants to be baptized." The church erupted in applause and praise to God. One thing I love about my pastor is that he didn't care what was going on and where he was; if someone wanted to accept Jesus Christ as Savior, he would stop and pray with that person. He did exactly what he would do on a Sunday morning when the invitation to Christ was extended.

I felt that I was doing the right thing, and I knew that the only way to get to experience Jesus more than I already have been was to welcome him into my heart. My grandmother was standing right by me, and beside her was my first Sunday school teacher (whom I was close to since being in her Sunday school class). My grandmother started to cry, but I saw that they weren't sad tears but happy tears. Then I looked out into the crowd and saw my mom. She wasn't mad at all; she was smiling so hard. I don't know if I'm correct, but it looked like she mouthed the words "I'm proud of you" while I was standing with the pastor. My pastor prayed with me. A girl my age came up and said she wanted to be baptized too. My pastor gave both of us a big hug and told us that we will be baptized the upcoming Tuesday evening before Bible study. My mom later told me that by walking to the pastor on my own and doing what I did showed that God was definitely working through me. She was proud that I allowed God to direct me. That Tuesday night, I walked up the steps to the baptismal pool. Most of my family was there, including my godmother (who at the time was my PE Coach in school).

I remember talking to the girl who got baptized with me, and she was really nice, which made things better for me because I was excited and nervous at the same time. Prior to the baptismal, I'm glad we practiced what was going to happen during the service because I thought I was going to mess up, but I didn't. I remember making it to the baptismal pool, and I couldn't believe that I was first. I had and still do have a huge fear of deep water. Nonetheless, I wasn't afraid because I knew everything was going to be alright. After my pastor opened up the service and spoke some words to the congregation, the time had arrived! He started singing, *Take me to the water, take me to the water, take me to the water, to be baptized.* After singing that verse twice, he reached up to me to step down, and I started walking down into the water. I remember looking out into the congregation and being amazed at how everybody looked like small ants from the baptismal pool. I sat down on the bench in the pool. I tried to place my feet behind the rail (so I wouldn't fall back), but I was too short. In my head, I was saying, Lord, please don't let me fall. After singing another verse of the song, he raised his right hand and shouted, "In obedience to his command and by your profession of Faith, I baptize you my brother, in the name of the Father, Son, and Holy Spirit." After that, he laid me back into the water, and even though he quickly brought me back up, once I went under, it's like time stood still for a second. It was absolutely incredible!

I remember afterward while drying off and putting on dry clothes, I was so excited that my dad (with a smile on his face) told me to calm down. I tried to but I couldn't. I was so very happy, and I knew that the choice I had made was for the best. I knew that my life would never be the same again. I could not wait to see what God had in store for my life. This was the beginning of something so great! Nevertheless, to every new journey, there are going to be some struggles.

CHAPTER 5

BEAR YOUR CROSS

(MARCH 19, 2000)

THIS IS THE FIRST of the services and messages I wish I had on video. I ended up being super happy purchasing the cassette tape a few years ago after having forgotten the date of the service. Sunday, March 19, 2000 is a Sunday I remember mostly because of the way my pastor demonstrated what it meant to carry your cross. It was a great service altogether, but that sermon was awesome. The sermon was based on the scripture in St. Mark Chapter 8.

"And when he had called the people unto him with his disciples also, he said unto them, Whosoever will come after me, let him deny himself, and take up his cross, and follow me."

Now being a kid, I didn't always get a full understanding, but I always got at least one thing about the sermon. But this Sunday, I got it completely. Listening to it on cassette tape reminds me so much of what I was feeling that day. It didn't really hit me until the part of the sermon when he was shouting. This is when I learned what taking up your cross means. It means that there are some things in life we are going to have to learn to deal with. There are some things we are going to have to learn how to go through in order to get to. Taking up your cross is not easy. It's not a walk in the park.

When you think of a physical cross, it is huge and heavy. When someone was sentenced to be crucified, they had to carry their cross to the place they were to be crucified at. Praise be to God for Jesus; He is here to help us. My pastor was on fire this particular Sunday. Now, don't get me wrong, he always taught awesome lessons and preached powerful sermons. God used him in an extra special way this particular Sunday. I remember him coming off the pulpit. I remember moving around trying to see what he was doing. I could clearly hear him but could not really see him. Then all of a sudden, I remember he was explaining bearing your cross, and what he did next blew my mind. He picked up the podium used for the welcome and announcements on the floor and started to carry it. While carrying it, he was continuing to preach. A light bulb went off in my head, and the Holy Spirit was moving extra heavy. I was doing all I could to see him in between all the people. Because I've always been a visual learner, this sermon really became more understandable for me, especially being a kid at the time. I'll never forget seeing so many people giving God praise and truly letting him have his way.

I remember that week following, I was sitting on my great grandfather's porch, and we were talking about the service. He showed me a pair of old school binoculars. The kind you had to insert the picture at the end on the binoculars then look through the lens. I hope I explained it correctly. My great grandfather showed me illustrations of Jesus carrying his cross to Calvary. I remember saying, "That's what pastor was talking about on Sunday." He replied, "That's right." I can't help but smile right now because this was one of those times that are special to me. Even to this day when I learn something new about Jesus Christ and that light bulb goes off in my head, I cannot help but smile and give God praise for his Word.

I got saved in 1999, but in 2000, I truly started to learn what it truly meant to trust and talk to Jesus. In June 2000, my great grandfather passed away.

CHAPTER 6

I Must Tell Jesus

(JUNE 2000)

IN JUNE 2000, my great grandfather passed away. Losing him was so hard for me. I couldn't believe he was gone. My great grandfather (whom everyone called Daddy) was a huge support for me. We did so much together. I would go with him to his church sometimes, and he would sometimes come to church with me and my parents. He knew about my calling and told me that one day, God's will would come to pass. I remember his church would only have service two or three Sundays out of the month. Every now and then when he stayed home because of his church not having service, I would stay with him.

I named this chapter "I Must Tell Jesus" for numerous reasons. This hymn really helped me during this particular time in my life. The words are something I can really relate to. The message in that hymn is so awesome. The hymn is also very reassuring because I know that Jesus can help, and Jesus alone. Those special Sundays when I would stay home with him and listen to Mt. Calvary on the radio were so special and exciting. As I'm writing this, I can still picture myself sitting on the edge of his bed with him listening to *"I Must Tell Jesus."* My first couple of years on this earth was with him mostly. When a family member picked on me, he always stood up for me. When I used to sing in his room or used to "preach" (God was in me at a young age), he was always telling everybody to be quiet and to listen. He always took me to get my haircut and most of the time would pick me up from school. We were always together doing stuff, and I learned so much from him. I knew he was sick but never realized that it was serious. It's like my world came crashing down in June 2000. I'll never forget being in the living room and hearing one of my relatives say that he's gone. I didn't go back in his room after that. Even as a child, I did not want to see him lying lifeless.

There was so much that I wanted to do in life, and the man I wanted to do it with was no longer here. I cried my tears and went outside to play. While waiting on the coroner and the funeral home to come, I watched my relatives say their goodbyes to my great grandfather. Each of them came out crying. As time passed, the coroner came and the funeral home came as well. I saw them put him in the back of the hearse. I never told nobody this, but as they brought him down the steps, I was so angry and heartbroken. In my head I was asking, "Why are you leaving me? It's not fair; you weren't supposed to go yet!" It was at that moment in which I realized that he really wasn't coming back. I couldn't do nothing else but cry. I was reminded of my favorite hymn, *"I Must Tell Jesus."* Soon after they took his body away, his pastor came to the house to pray with us. I cannot remember who I told, but I told somebody, "I want to sing *'I Must Tell Jesus'*." I was told to wait until after the pastor prays. After Daddy's pastor prayed, my relative told the pastor that I want to sing *"I Must Tell Jesus."* The Pastor agreed, and before I could even start, I was already breaking down. We all gathered in a circle in the living room and I started to sing: *"I must tell Jesus, all of my trials, I cannot bear these burdens alone."* After that, I could barely continue, but the pastor helped me continue with the song while holding my hand very tightly. The Pastor sang, *"In my distress, he kindly will help me, he ever loves and cares for his own."* Everybody was crying, and I knew that things were never going to be the same after that. It was extra hard to bear because he died a month after his birthday and a few days before Father's Day.

What really shook me and made me realize this was a very serious situation was my mother. Up until that time, I had never seen my mom cry. At his funeral, I'll never forget seeing my mom cry. I haven't had the blessing of becoming a father yet, but as a son, one thing that pains me is to see my mother cry. All these years later, I will never forget the feeling I had. I wasn't concerned for me; I was concerned for my mom. As a young child who never seen his mother cry, I just wanted her to be happy. What I'm about to say is true facts . . . I wanted to walk up to the casket and say "Daddy, please come back. We need you." My grandmother wasn't crying. That was her father, and she wasn't crying. Something she told me made me realize that everything was going to be alright. She said, "Daddy is in a better place and he want us to keep on living." I didn't understand those words at the time, but as time went on, I understood.

To this day, *"I Must Tell Jesus"* is still my go-to hymn when

I'm feeling down. Let me correct that . . . *"I Must Tell Jesus"* is a hymn I go to in the good, bad, sad, and happy times. I knew I had to keep on living and not let anything hold me back. Jesus was leading me all the way, and I knew that I had to do what he wanted me to do. By the time September came, I knew it was time for me to do something I've been waiting to do for a while; become an usher at church.

CHAPTER 7

GOD'S DOORKEEPER

(SEPTEMBER 2000)

BEFORE I START TALKING about how I became a junior usher, I have to tell this story from New Member Orientation the year prior. This was a few months before I got saved. They sent the kids into another room for a special lesson. Now remember, I was seven at the time and wasn't involved in a ministry yet. The teacher asked everyone to say their name and say what ministries they were a part of. I looked around and noticed I was the only one in there who wasn't involved in anything. I didn't show it, but I was panicking on the inside. By the time it was my turn, I said my name and then said, "I'm not in anything. I just watch." Some had this blank look on their face, and some laughed. At the time, I gave an honest answer, and I wasn't embarrassed. Of course, if I was older, I would have given a better answer, but I did my best. For some reason, every time I think about when I became an usher, I think of that story. Now back to September 2000.

A few months after my great grandfather died, I felt that I should continue to pursue God. I knew he would want me to move on and continue staying focused on God. I remember growing up in church, seeing my dad and his father ushering. Becoming an usher was something I wanted to do, and I knew that it was something that needed to happen. I'll never forget one Sunday, after Sunday school, I was in the hallway before service and saw my pastor and his wife come down the hallway from the activity room. The hallway was packed, and a lot of people were talking to them. But that didn't stop me at all. Like I did before, I went to my pastor about wanting to become an usher. Somehow, someway, I made it to him through the crowd. I went straight to him, and when he saw me, he said, "Hey, son, how are you?" Very bluntly, I said, "I'm good. I want to become an usher."

One thing I love about my pastor is that he never asked any questions. He said okay and got me connected. Now I know some of you may say, "Well, he should have asked your parents first." My parents saw what was happening and were very proud of me being bold and wanting to serve in the church. They could have stopped me, but they didn't. I ushered at my home church for ten years. I learned a lot from being an usher. I remember I used to have a fit on Sunday mornings when I had to usher. That's because I would do my best to put my badge on straight, but it would not stay straight. It was a struggle that was aggravating but very funny now.

My favorite place to usher was in the choir stand. I loved being close to the choir and pulpit. I felt a special connection with God from there. From the choir stand, you could see the whole sanctuary. Seeing people praise God and letting the Holy

Spirit move was an incredible sight and still is to this day for me. There was plenty of moments I had with God during my time as an usher. I believe the reason my attention was more focused on God during the Sunday's I ushered was that it made me come out of my comfort zone. You are going to hear about two of my moments with God while ushering in Chapters 10, 12, and 15. I didn't always usher on the choir stand. I ushered at different posts in the church. Even though I was out of my comfort zone, it's like my focus was more on what was going on during service and what my pastor was saying.

I'll never forget the junior usher meetings, gatherings, anniversaries, and the musicals with the adult ushers. One thing that breaks my heart is that the three original junior usher advisors are no longer with us. They are truly missed, and I'll never forget their dedication and their love to the junior ushers. I'll never forget the lessons I received during my ushering days at Mt. Calvary.

I will save the rest of my comments about the usher ministry for Chapter 23. I have a funny story about the very first Sunday I marched with the ushers during the main offering. I'm laughing in my head just thinking about it.

CHAPTER 8

Oh Lord, How Excellent

(DECEMBER 17, 2000)

THIS IS ANOTHER SUNDAY I wish I had on video because it was a powerful service. You would think October would be my only favorite month because of my birthday. But December is my favorite month, not only because it's the month set aside to celebrate the birth of our Lord and Savior Jesus Christ, but a lot of great memories come from the month of December. Even until this day, great things seem to still happen a lot for me in the month of December. I was ordained in December and passed my GED test in December. Something else happened in December, but I will talk about that in Chapter 13.

This particular Sunday in 2000 is one that sticks out in my mind. Every service you attend, your main focus ought to be hearing the Word. But there are a few things that happen before getting to the Word, one of which is hearing the choir minister. Now I have a whole chapter in this book about Mt. Calvary's choirs and music ministry. I want you to know that

Mt. Calvary has some of the most anointed choirs I've ever heard minister in song. I'm not even saying that because this is my home church. This Sunday was a powerful service. I remember the service being at the halfway point. I remember hearing a song that I had never heard before. The song was "Emmanuel." Not the one by Norman Hutchins, this song is by the Mississippi Mass Choir. I didn't know what Emmanuel meant at the time, but I remember how excited the whole church got when they heard the song.

I was having one of those experiences where I was looking around and seeing how the Holy Spirit was touching people. You never know what someone is going through or what they need. I just knew the Holy Spirit was truly moving and touching a lot of people. After the choir sang "Emmanuel," the sanctuary was filled with shouts of praise to God for his son Jesus Christ. My pastor actually said right before the choir sang the next song, "Emmanuel, God with Us." I remember hearing that and noticing how he said it. Not too long afterward, I was told that Emmanuel meant "God with us," and that it was in the Bible.

> *"Behold, a virgin shall be with child, and shall bring forth a son, and they shall call his name Emmanuel, which being interpreted is, God with us."*
> MATTHEW 1:23

That was another light bulb moment for me. Now I thought the praise couldn't get any higher, but it did. The next song was *"Perfect Praise (Oh Lord How Excellent)."* My eyes were big during the entire song. The song is actually based on Psalm 34.

A true Gospel song is a song that comes straight from the Word. I'm not knocking any song that comes out that's inspirational or encouraging but that's really what a Gospel song is. The only reason I'm even mentioning this is looking back at this particular Sunday still proves to me how powerful God's Word really is. Even my pastor ended up singing a little bit of the "Yes Lord" chant. This whole service was so powerful, but honestly, that middle portion of the service truly was my sermon that day. A lot of services and sermons made me hungrier to get closer to Jesus. There have been plenty of times I've left church full and excited for all I had received. It's one thing to have an experience with Jesus, but to leave a service full, encouraged, and excited is what matters. I definitely want to walk out different than the way I entered in. Something I used to hear a lot growing up at Mt. Calvary is my pastor saying, "We are on a transformative journey!" That's something I carry with me to this day because that's what the Christian is. We are not conforming to the world journey, it's a "transformative journey." This Sunday definitely was great.

The year 2000 had its challenges, but it was a great year. The start of 2001 is one that stands out to me I was asked to do a skit that was totally out of my comfort zone.

CHAPTER 9

Pastor Anniversary Skit

(February 2001)

I WAS APPROACHED in late December 2000 or early January 2001 to do a skit for our pastor's upcoming twenty-eighth pastoral anniversary. Basically, one of the anniversary tribute programs was going to be put together like a church service. If you are going to do that, you need someone to "preach." Now it has been over twenty years since this has happened. I will never get over how I was chosen over so many other kids my age who were more talkative and active than I was at the time. Looking back on this program in 2001 and another youth program in which I played the preacher in 2007, these programs really was God showing me what was to come. Because, in my opinion, there were a lot more kids my age that could have done the part better, but I was chosen. I know it had to be God behind it all. I thank God that my parents were never the type to force me to do anything when it came to church. They would talk with me and encourage me, but I was never forced. One lesson they taught me is to always give stuff a try. So that's what I did. I gave it a try. The person who put the skit together was someone who sang on the choir. She was an author and also was very creative. I can still remember seeing the script and how professional it looked.

As a kid, I was nervous. I remember how glad I was that I didn't have to memorize the script, which made it easy the night of the program because I never had to look up during the skit. I only remember having one rehearsal with the person who wrote the play. The rest of the times I practiced at home with my parents and my grandmother. Let me point out some things I was told I had to do by the lady who wrote the skit. I was asked not to get my hair cut because during the skit, there were a few times I would need to pat my hair. Now my pastor had a huge afro, which to me was his signature. Everyone has at least one thing special about them. My pastor has a lot. But if you had to choose anything outside of his calling and what he does that describes him, his afro is going to be named at some point. When he preaches, he pats his afro. I didn't have an afro for this skit, but I had enough hair to get the job done. I was told if I wanted to get my hair cut, I could wear a wig. I immediately said, "I'll wait to get a haircut." I made sure I got my hair cut before the pastor anniversary service. Also, I was told that I would have to keep a serious look on my face because even though it was a skit, I was imitating my pastor and I had to "stay in character." We laughed because we all knew that was going to be a challenge.

The skit was funny because it pointed out a lot about our pastor that really described him while he is preaching. Honestly, even though it was a skit, the message was well put together. It even got a few amens.

So let me tell you about the night of the skit, February 13, 2001. The activity room at Mt. Calvary was so packed to the point there were people standing. In the beginning of the video, you can see me looking around. I was nervous, but I was also looking for my cue to go get ready. I must say this: that whole program was awesome! Everything was so well put together. It was a great night of tribute to our pastor and a great night of fellowship with each other. Everything on the program was great! The Children and Youth Choir sang, poetry was recited, the pantomime team performed, and other ministries presented tributes to our pastor. It was a great night! It came time for my skit. I got the cue during the program to step out and get ready. I was super nervous because I knew that there was going to be people looking at me, and I knew kids my age would be laughing (not in a bad way, though). I went in the music room, and the lady who wrote the skit handed me this beautiful silver robe. My eyes lit up. I was excited to put it on. I wish I still had it because it looked that good to me.

I remember walking out of the music room and waiting in the hallway before I was told to go in. There were already people who saw me because either they were in the hallway or standing near the door. Every comment that was made, my response was a smile. I was very shy and quiet at this time. This was totally out of my comfort zone. I remember everyone stood up and they started singing, *"Blessed Assurance."* Now one thing about my pastor, his voice travels. I can remember hearing his voice over everyone. It was like Sunday morning up in there. Then it was time for the moment of truth. I was told to go in and sit in the middle chair at the front. The front of the activity room was set up like the pulpit, and I sat in the preacher's chair, which was the middle. Well, actually, I didn't get a chance to sit down in that chair until after the skit because when I walked in, everyone was still singing *"Blessed Assurance."* At Mt. Calvary, there were certain hymns that the congregation would stand on and *"Blessed Assurance"* was one of them.

As I was walking towards the preacher's chair, I heard laughter, and I heard a lot of people saying "AWWWWW." My main focus was getting to the front. Thank God there were a group of guys standing in front of me, blocking me from seeing everybody. When the hymn was over and I approached the podium, I heard nothing but laughter and giggles (good laughter and giggles). The microphone was lowered for me, and I remember trying to peek out into the audience, but the podium partially blocked my view, which made the whole skit for me easier. It was smooth from there. I imitated my pastor to the best of my ability, and I remember having so much fun doing it. There were a lot of times I almost laughed, but I kept it together. Even at the end of the program, my pastor got in a joke saying, "I don't want to walk off without acknowledging the pastor." Everyone started laughing, and all I did was smile. I remember after the benediction; everyone approached me telling me how great of a job I did. Even kids my age were coming to me telling me I did great and shaking my hand. My pastor gave me one of the biggest hugs and told me how proud he was of me. I didn't think I did anything that big at the time, but seeing people's reaction told the story.

It's amazing how this skit really taught me about how important it is to step outside of your comfort zone. It's funny looking back on this night and looking around now in the present as a Reverend. God has his ways of preparing you for what's ahead. Always be ready to be used by God. You never know when He's going to present a special task for you. If He brought you to it, He will see you through it.

CHAPTER 10

GLORY!

(AUGUST 12, 2001)

I'LL NEVER FORGET one Sunday in 2001. It was August 12, 2001. This is another service I wish I had on video, and I actually purchased the audio cassette tape a few short years later after forgetting the date of the service. I stumbled across the date while looking through old notes I took in 2001. This service was great, but the ending is what really blessed me. I was ushering on the choir stand on this particular Sunday, and I'm so glad I was up there to see all that happened. My pastor was preaching, and you can just feel God moving through the church.

When he opened the doors of the church, while the choir was singing a hymn, he invited people to come to the altar to give God praise. The choir was singing:

"Down at the cross where my Savior died
Down where for cleansing from I cried,

There to my heart was the blood applied
Glory to his name!
Glory to his name (precious name)
Glory to his name (precious name)
There to my heart was the blood applied
Glory to his name!"

The whole altar was packed full of people praising God. I was ushering on the side of the choir stand right next to the musicians. I can tell God was moving through them as well. After the song had ended, the praise did not stop. The musicians had kind of stopped playing. All you can see and hear is people giving God praise. The Holy Spirit had fallen down in that place. It was like the day of Pentecost. Even my pastor had stopped talking for a minute. Then all of a sudden, my pastor started back shouting. He was shouting, "GLORY, GLORY TO HIS NAME!" It's something about not only giving God praise, but when you think of the goodness of Jesus, you cannot help but to give praise.

As I looked out, I realized that these people were in a moment; they were having an experience with the Holy Spirit. Then all of a sudden, I heard the musicians starting to play some shouting music, and I remember standing in complete awe what was happening. Up to that point, I had seen God move a lot, but that particular Sunday is something that has stuck with me since then. That particular Sunday, I was ushering, and I myself had, just by standing there looking in complete awe, an unforgettable experience with God.

This was my first time on the choir stand seeing God move

like that from that view. Then the service ended with the choir singing "Give Glory to God Saints." This was another one of those Sundays I left church full, excited, and hungrier for a closer relationship with Jesus Christ.

CHAPTER 11

WHEN THE HEAT IS ON!

(MARCH 3, 2002)

THERE ARE THREE SERMONS I heard at my church that are my absolute favorites still to this day. The interesting fact is those sermons were all delivered in 2002. One of those I'm going to talk about in this chapter. The next one I'm going to talk about a little bit in the next chapter, and the third one I'm going to talk about in Chapter 13.

The first sermon I want to talk about was one my pastor preached entitled *"When the Heat Is On"* from Sunday, March 3, 2002. The service was great, and leading up to the message, I remember having this feeling that something was going to go down. The sermon was based on the fiery furnace about Shadrach, Meshach, and Abednego. I just kept having this feeling that something was going to happen. I knew God was up to something. I am going to admit that while the message was being preached, I was more focused on what God was up to than trying to take notes. My mom ended up purchasing the cassette tape after service, so I was able to get something more out of it later that day.

By the time my pastor had reached the end of his sermon, that feeling intensified. This message was so different for me because the story he was preaching about has always been a story that fascinated me early on in life. I was able to relate to it. Hearing him preach about it brought light on it. I remember that at one point he was finished, but he kept going. I remember standing up and looking on because I really was enjoying what I was hearing and I was enjoying seeing the Holy Spirit move. The Holy Spirit was moving so heavy. My pastor called for anybody to come forth and say, "God is good." Suddenly, the altar filled with so many people. I remember a heavy praise erupted in the sanctuary.

I had the biggest grin on my face because of all that was happening. There has always been something about the move of God in church that excites me. I have to testify really quickly before finishing this chapter. When God is moving, whether you're at church, home, or wherever, don't miss out on embracing His presence. I love embracing His presence. A few minutes after that praise erupted, my pastor started singing "Take My Hand, Precious Lord." That was the perfect song to close out that powerful message.

Later that day, when listening to the sermon, what I got from it is something I will never forget. "When things in life gets hard, God will always make a way." A few short years afterward, I was able to purchase the video. I'm so glad I have video footage from that service. *When the heat is on* sermon will definitely be one of those messages I will hold close to my heart for the rest of my life.

CHAPTER 12

Yes, Lord, Yes

(October 13, 2002)

THE YEAR 2002 was a year in which God started using me in an incredible way. I'll go more in depth into that in Chapter 13. On Sunday, August 4, 2002, one of the daughters of the house preached a sermon entitled *"It Ain't Over Yet."* The title itself really describes the whole sermon. She brought a powerful Word. It's definitely one of my favorites. I still listen to the service and sermon on cassette tape till this day.

Now, let me get into October 2002. I remember this Sunday very well. Also, I often go back and watch this Sunday Service on video. I was ushering on this day. At first, I was assigned to a door position. I recall watching the praise team sing. One of the former choir members had come back for that Sunday and she sang "I'm running for my life." I remember being so happy hearing that song again because it had been a while since I had last heard it. Right before service fully started, I moved to an aisle position to usher. This position placed me on the aisle near my family. It wasn't often that I ushered so close to them, and when I did, I would get so happy for some reason. The service was wonderful. In the middle of the service, the choir ministered a song called, "Yes, Lord, Yes."

"I'll say, "Yes, Lord, yes"
To Your will and to your way
I'll say, "Yes, Lord, yes"
I will trust You and obey
When your Spirit speaks to me
With my whole heart I'll agree
And my answer will be, "Yes, Lord, yes"

This was the first time I've ever heard that song. I was happy listening to the song. Right after the song was over, I noticed a huge shift in the worship service. It took me years to understand what happened. The Holy Spirit rested upon the people in the sanctuary. One of the daughters of the house stepped up to the pulpit to continue on with the service, but the Holy Spirit was moving heavy in the place. The choir directress grabbed the microphone and started singing the *"Yes Lord"* chant. The *"Yes Lord"* chant always does something to me. Just like *"I Must Tell Jesus,"* this chant always fills me up. After she ministered that chant, everywhere I looked, people were shouting. Now keep in mind, I was ten years old (about to turn eleven that coming week), and I was short. I was looking up and around at everything. My mind was blown at how God was moving during this service. I had seen the Holy Spirit move plenty of times before, but this was different for some reason. I kept turning my head over to the musician corner. I knew that they were about to start playing some shouting music. I remember thinking to myself that if they didn't play shouting music soon, the congregation was going to make their own shouting music. I'm laughing so hard right now because that's exactly what I thought while I was ushering.

Unexpectedly, the music started and the whole church went in! All I could do was clap my hands and look. I was just a young boy watching the Holy Spirit move. I tell you this: I love seeing the Holy Spirit move. Whether it's in church or out in the world, it's a beautiful and holy sight (I'm not talking about just shouting and praise dancing either). After the praise break, things calmed down but not fully. Offering was taken up, and my pastor ministered the hymn "Father, I Stretch My Hands to Thee" before his sermon.

The sermon topic was *"What Believers Have Through Christ."* The one thing I received from the message was, "I'm so glad I have Jesus." I didn't understand everything he said, but I understood enough to know that I'm glad I have Jesus in my life. The Pastor preached his heart out. The choir ministered two songs during the invitation to Christ: *"I Still Have Joy"* and *"This Joy I Have the World Didn't Give It to Me."* Those songs went great with the sermon.

I thought the praise was never going to stop, and honestly, I didn't want it to. The former choir director who had just become a minister started singing a little bit of *"It's No Secret What God Can Do."* Looking back to this Sunday always gets me happy, and it means more to me now than it did back then.

My birthday was that Wednesday. This Sunday made me more excited for my birthday. Little did I know that age eleven was going to be a very special year for me. It would be the official start of my ministry.

CHAPTER 13

WORK WITH WHAT YOU GOT

(DECEMBER 2002)

IN 2000, I was given a karaoke machine for Christmas by my mother and grandmother. My great-grandfather passed months prior. He was the first person to know about my calling. He always told me to follow God no matter what. Back then, having a karaoke machine was a must have. Mine had a radio on it, and it was a two-sided cassette player. I really started loving it once I started learning how to record on it. I did some recordings on it in 2002, but little did I know that my life was about to change. I remember one thing: I got tired of hearing adults tell me as a kid that I don't know what I want and that I don't understand what I'm talking about. There may be some truth to that. However, I knew that God was definitely in me. I wanted to learn more and become a better Christian. Not perfect, but better; there's a difference.

Something that has followed me into my adult years is I do what God wants, and it's always going to work out for my good.

Just because others don't understand or approve, that's their problem, not mine. On December 1, 2002, my home church pastor preached a sermon titled *"It's going to be alright."* That sermon ignited a fire in me; it's definitely one of my favorite sermons I heard him preach. That sermon led me to December 14, 2002, when I started my ministry. I didn't get licensed until 2016 and ordained until 2021, but I always consider December 14, 2002 as my official start in ministry. This was before social media, streaming services, smart devices, etc.

On a Saturday morning as a kid, all you had to do was watch TV, go outside and play, go somewhere, or make up your own fun. Well, this particular morning, I grabbed my cap and gown robe that was given to me, my Bible, and my microphone. I found a cassette tape and put it into my karaoke machine. Once I hit that play and record button, that was it. The tape kept messing up at first, but I kept trying to record until it worked. I used snippets from the service on December 1st on that first recording. Once I finished it, I gave it to my mom, then she gave it to my grandmother, then my grandmother played it to people she knew. To my surprise, people were actually being blessed by it. I did another recording on Christian Eve. On Christmas day I received bags full of the three pack sixty-minute cassette tapes from my mom and grandmother for Christmas. This was the start of my ministry, which is today an award-winning podcast. Those cassette tapes lasted for the rest of 2002 and most of 2003.

I have seen Jesus change lives, save souls, and so much more! It wasn't always easy, and I always didn't do everything right in life. I took what I did very seriously. I was always picked on, judged, persecuted, and rejected. When I reached my late teens and early twenties, people were telling me that I needed to stop what I was doing and grow up. But I did not stop doing what God was telling me to do. I never worried about what I didn't have. I always have worked with what I got.

Things will happen when they are supposed to. I do my best to always think and pray big and not little. We must focus on point A before trying to get to point B. My ministry has been running strong for Jesus for over two decades now. I'm nowhere near stopping! I may write a separate book about this one day because this is a testimony itself. I believe one thing that amazes me despite what I have experienced: God has never left me, and I have never completely abandoned God. It hasn't always been easy for me.

CHAPTER 14

LIFE GETS REAL

(MARCH 2005)

LIFE STARTED TO GET VERY REAL for me in March 2005. I have come out of my shell so very much over the years. But back when I was younger, I was super quiet, shy, and I stayed to myself. I was picked on and bullied a lot, not because I did anything but because of me being me. I have always loved the Lord, but when I hit my teen years, I started to realize how unpopular that was. I used to put too much focus on fitting in and making friends, to the point that my relationship with God was affected. To make things worse, my health started to become a problem. I have struggled for so many years with anxiety and depression. I praise God that presently this isn't an issue no more, but it took me years to get to where I'm at today.

In March 2005, my health problems started. My life was already kind of hard due to bullying, but my health issues made it so much worse. My anxiety and depression were so bad at times that it caused me to pass out. I have been accused of faking my health issues and was rejected by people because of it. Some people got a sick obsession of picking at my condition. It's a sad thing when others get joy out of your misery. There were plenty of times I wanted to die and take my life. I felt so worthless. I didn't have no clue how God was going to get me through what I was experiencing. The only person who knew a hundred percent of what I was going through physically, mentally, and spiritually was God. I was trying to fit in with kids at school, which didn't work at all. I was trying to be someone I wasn't or could never be. I had just turned thirteen years old months prior, and my life was becoming much more real to me.

Presently, my life is so much better, but back during that time, I was barely holding on. It's so amazing how through everything that was happening, I still found happiness in Jesus and going to church. That summer, my pastor started a sermon series on Love. My favorite sermon from the series was Love Endures, on September 11, 2005.

CHAPTER 15

Love Endures

(September 2005)

Sunday, september 11, 2005 was a great worship service at church. Honestly, this was the first time ever I broke down in church. For me personally, the two parts in the worship service that blessed me was when the choir sang *"Peace Be Still"* and the sermon *"Love Endures."* This was the Sunday before the church anniversary. Back then, each member was asked to submit an inspirational quote that goes with our anniversary theme to be posted on the wall in the church hallway. My pastor set aside time in the middle of the worship service for members to complete their inspirational quote form. During this time, he asked the musicians to play *"Peace Be Still."* I was ushering and helping collect the forms.

I had heard the song *"Peace Be Still"* before a few times. This Sunday and a Sunday back in August 2003 are the two times this song stood out to me as a kid. I've learned that the song is based on *Mark 8:35–41.* These scriptures helped me to understand the message behind the song during a rough time in my life with my health. Even though it wasn't until sometime after this when I learned the message behind the song, I felt reassured.

Now this happened in the middle of the service. The sermon that was preached truly overwhelmed me. It overwhelmed me to the point that my grandfather and my father had to come see about me on my usher post. I was ushering on the choir stand and ended up sitting with them in the congregation for the rest of the service. That love series my pastor preached was awesome! The Sunday before was great, but this Sunday really hit me. The subject *"Love Endures"* speaks for itself. By that point, I was going through a lot health wise and in school. I was barely hanging on. The sermon was a reminder of how much I am loved by the Lord. Even though I was having a hard time and felt alone, I knew that Jesus loves me. God used my pastor in a special way this particular Sunday. The Holy Spirit was moving so much during the sermon that my pastor ended up doing an altar call and the praises to God went up even more. I couldn't stay seated. Abruptly, the musicians began playing shouting music. I remember being over taken by the Holy Spirit. I didn't get my dance on for Jesus but my hands were clapping like crazy. I couldn't contain my praise!

That praise break lasted a few minutes, and I remember feeling so good and happy. Quickly, I became overwhelmed. That's when my grandfather and father came to get me. When they were consoling me, I could hear my pastor open the doors of the church and the choir started to sing, *"The Vision (Write the Vision)."* I read the book of Habakkuk a few years after this, so I didn't have a full understanding of this song at the time. I love to hear it to this day, but the part that always stands out to me is *"If the Lord said it, you can count on it, He will do just want he said!"* This is a song I grew up on; those few words always stand out.

On September 11, 2005, I knew what I wanted and needed, and God knew. I knew that someday I was going to be at a place in life where I would be at peace, no health issues, and be happy with who I was. The love of God truly endures! From that Sunday in 2005 through 2006, a lot happened in my life. I was still dealing with a lot, but by the time November 2006 arrived, things in my life started to improve. It all started at Choir Day 2006 on Sunday, November 19, 2006.

CHAPTER 16

CHOIR DAY

(NOVEMBER 2006)

CHAPTERS 17 AND 24 will go more in depth about the choirs and music ministry however, I had to do a chapter about Choir Day 2006 by itself. One thing I wanted to do is sing on the choir and play the drums at some point. I have always loved giving God praise through singing and playing the drums. God was truly leading me in that direction. Choir Day 2006 was the night God told me that it's time to move forward with that. Honestly, I won't be able to go into detail about everything that took place because it's just so much. I remember walking into Mt. Calvary and saying to myself, "Something is about to go down." I just felt that God had something wonderful in store for those who were in attendance.

The Children & Youth Choir kicked off the first part of the program. I was so filled up by their ministry through song, and that was just the first half. By the time we reached the second half, I was wondering what else could God be up to?

The combined adult choirs made their way to the choir stand. They opened with a great song. It had the church rocking with praise. I remember smiling so hard during this song. I guess I was just in an extra happy mood. The second song they ministered was *"Total Praise."* The choir has ministered this song ever since it first came out in the late 90s. It had been I think, four years since I had last heard them sing it. *"Total Praise"* has a beautiful intro; it stands out. It prepares you for worship. When I heard that intro, I knew that a huge worship moment was about to take place. I'm a type of worshipper who loves to truly worship. However, there are times I just sit back and soak everything in. Seeing others worship the Lord always has fascinated me. As the choir ministered, I looked around and seen true worship take place. I felt the presence of the Holy Spirit; it was such a wonderful moment. This moment still stands out today because it gave me so much peace while I was going through so much pain and stress. By the time they were finished ministering *"Total Praise,"* I was done. I could've gone home because I was so full and received so much.

The final part of the program was a music melody of *"Take Me Back, God Is, When God Dips His Love in My Heart, and Ride This Train."* This melody was a wonderful way to end such a Spirit filled program. I remember when they ministered *"God Is,"* my mind went straight back to when I was younger watching one of the choir members who had passed away ministered that song. After he passed, I had heard it ministered a few times. But this particular time took me back to when he used to minister it during my early childhood. The message behind that song always hits me and makes me realize what God truly means to me. The young man who led it at Choir Day 2006 really put his all into it. I'm laughing now because I remember wishing it could have been a little bit longer.

By the end of Choir Day 2006, God told me that it was time to do something I had been wanting to do for a long time. I had concerns due to my depression and anxiety, but I didn't let that stop me. I talked with my pastor, and after I talked to him, in 2007, I joined the choir and music ministry.

CHAPTER 17

Joining the Choir & Music Ministry

(MARCH 2007–DECEMBER 2008)

JOINED THE Children & Youth Mass Choir in March 2007. I ushered on second Sundays and sang in the choir on the fourth Sunday. The only time I had sung on the choir is when my pastor used to call all the men to come to the choir stand and sing with the male chorus during the Father/Son/Big Brother Fellowship Hour every June. I felt so happy when that happened, but now here I am as an official choir member. I was nervous and stiff; I knew this was going to be a process. What I mean by stiff is that I barely clapped my hands and I would barely move. I was just so nervous, and I knew it would be a process loosening up. The part that stands out for me during my first Sunday on the choir was when we ministered *"Do Not Pass Me By."* The way the Holy Spirit was moving was different for me because I was singing on the choir and knowing that this was something I was going to do every fourth Sunday.

It felt good knowing that singing on the choir every fourth Sunday was going to be another way to praise and worship the Lord at church. For me, it was the start of me coming out my shell and becoming more open to praise and worship God at church.

I've never told no one this, but singing on the choir at Mt. Calvary was like therapy for me. I don't think I would have made it through all I went through in the following years in school or life without singing on the choir. By June 2007, I started playing the drums in church. My first choir rehearsal with one of the adult choirs was the Friday before the second Sunday. Lord have mercy, that rehearsal still gives me chills all these years later. Mt. Calvary's choir rehearsals felt like church more than choir rehearsal. But this rehearsal always stands out. This was around the time Luther Barnes' song *"Spirit Fall Down"* first came out. The way this song was rehearsed was so Spirit filled and eye opening.

The former choir director who became a minister was at this rehearsal, and he helped teach this song. It was one thing to watch the choir minister on Sunday mornings, but seeing them rehearse was another story. By the time the parts were taught and words of preparation were given, the choir went over the entire song. They rehearsed it straight through without stopping or making a mistake. This song took up most of the rehearsal. After going over the parts and singing the song, it turned into a worship moment. I was sitting there just lost for words. I absolutely was amazed at what I was experiencing. I must point out that the only reason I was there that night was not to play the drums but to sit and see how the other choirs rehearsed. Up until that point, I only had been to the Children

& Youth Mass Choir Rehearsal. Now every choir rehearsal has something special about it. But one thing I can say is the Holy Spirit truly was in the midst. One more thing I must point out about this rehearsal: one of the former choir members was in town and ended up ministering a song he always uses to sing, *"I've Seen God Work."* My Lord, even in his late 70s at the time, he ministered that song so wonderfully. He went home to be with the Lord in 2020. It was a joy to see him sing that song that night because it had been a while since I last heard him minister it. This rehearsal is still to this day one of my top three choir rehearsals I've ever attended.

I played my first song on the drums on the third Sunday (Father's Day) during the invitation to Christ. The hymn was *"Is Your All on The Altar?"* I remember going to the drum set and being so nervous because this was not me playing the drums at home. I was actually playing in a church service during a very special and important part of the service. I just focused on the song and asked God to guide me. I did not want to mess up what God was doing in that moment. The last thing I wanted to happen is messing up and that mess up ending up distracting someone from coming to Christ. But everything turned out fine. I remember feeling calm after the first verse. A lot of people didn't know I knew how to play the drums until that Sunday.

I'm going to share this last part about playing the drums at Mt. Calvary even though it happened a year later. On the first Sunday in December 2008, I was super happy to hear my pastor sing my favorite hymn, *"I Must Tell Jesus."* I ended up being on the drums during that moment. I absolutely was excited to play the song on the drums. It had been a few years since my pastor had ministered that hymn. To be able to hear that hymn and play it really made me happy. He ministered it at a time when I needed to hear it. I was experiencing a lot during that time.

I sang in the choir and was a part of the music ministry the last five years that I was a member at Mt. Calvary. I will never forget those years; I learned a lot, and it really was therapy for me. I want to tell you another story from 2007. I cannot continue to writing this book without talking about the Sunday I ministered my first song in church.

CHAPTER 18

Jesus, You're the Center of My Joy

(September 2007)

In order to fully understand this chapter, I must go back to late August 2007. The music coordinator asked the choir and music ministry to submit songs they would like to possibly hear sang for the church anniversary during the 11:00 a.m. worship service on the third Sunday in September. I submitted the song, *"Standing on the Promises"* (James Bignon version) and *"Center of My Joy."* Those songs stood out because they were two of my favorites and still are. I really wanted to hear them, and they were chosen. During the rehearsal leading up to the church anniversary, God spoke to me and told me to volunteer to sing "Center Of My Joy." Now I had went to the music coordinator and expressed to her that I wanted to try to lead a song in the future. I had rehearsed "Oh Happy Day" with another choir member at a rehearsal earlier in September so I'm thinking it was going to happen in due time. However, God had other things in mind, and it caught me off guard. During the rehearsal, I got up and went to the music coordinator and told her I wanted to give *"Center of My Joy"* a try, and she said yes. The only time I have sung this song was at home, but I never ever wanted to sing it at church because I just thought I could not lead that song properly and I was still dealing with the thought of ministering in front of everyone at church. I ended up singing the song, and it went well, which surprised me. Everyone was clapping and telling me I did good. I ended up singing with the choir that Sunday, but I didn't actually minister the song until the fourth Sunday.

I rehearsed *"Center of My Joy"* again, this time with the Children & Youth Mass Choir. I was even more nervous because I sang it around kids my age. A few of them were present the week prior because the church anniversary was a mixture of every choir at Mt. Calvary. But this was in front of the entire Children & Youth Mass Choir; it turned out wonderfully. When the fourth Sunday arrived, I remember walking onto the choir stand and seeing a lot of people. Now there was always people there, but there were more people there than usual. Then it got more real during the welcome and announcements when the choir director pointed at me and whispered, "You're next." I was calm on the outside, but I was freaking out on the inside. It's funny now, but back then I was trying to keep myself together. My nerves were shot, and I was asking God to just have his way in me. I just wanted to minister this song and do it the way God wanted.

After the announcements, I got up and went to the microphone. I had the words with me only in case my nervousness caused me to forgot the words. It's amazing how I battled depression and anxiety but have been able to get up in front of people and minister. Normally, the person leading the song starts off the song. Thank God, the choir director had the choir start off. Thank God she did that because that helped me to calm down a lot. By the time I started the first verse, I freaked out because the sound was so different in the sanctuary than it was in the music room. However, I didn't let that stop me from ministering. My voice was changing at the time and would often make this squeaking noise when I sang. It only happened once in the song, but I didn't even notice it until I listened back to the recording. Honestly, I was completely taken over by the Holy Spirit during that song. I don't remember more about the reaction of the congregation, but I do remember my pastor writing something, and he ended up stopping what he was doing and looked at me sing. The former choir director was on the pulpit that Sunday, and I remember him being one of the people who used to minister that song. It's funny to me now because when I recommended that song, I was expecting him to minister it, not me. The only things I remember saying to myself while singing was "Don't cry and "Keep it together" because the Holy Spirit was moving heavy.

After the song was over, the choir director hugged me tight. I walked back to my section, and everyone was saying how good I did. The tears of joy and praise was at the edge of my eyes, but I held it together. I knew God was pleased, and I was very happy. So many people came to me and told me how much I blessed them; that's what matters most. Singing for the Lord is not only a form of praise and worship to God, but it's about ministry as well! The song *"Center of My Joy"* is a classic and has been a part of my life a lot. It's definitely a song that fits me and my testimony even to this day. I was able to contain myself on this Sunday. However, three years later, during the 11:00 a.m. worship service on the third Sunday in February, I couldn't contain myself no longer.

CHAPTER 19

I Can Go to God in Prayer

(February 2010)

Between 2007 and 2010, I had grown a lot but still had a lot more to learn as a young man in Christ. I had felt the presence of the Holy Spirt move, but as I got older, it got more intense (in a very good way). The Holy Spirit does make us move and shout, but the Holy Spirit guides, protects, and convicts us. On Sunday, February 21, 2010, I couldn't contain my praise no more. At home, I always worshipped and praised God, but at church, I really never let loose completely in praise up to this point. As you all have read in previous chapters, I have had moments of praise and worship and have shed tears of joy and praise. But by this time in my life, I had been through a lot more in life and was still facing a few issues. This Sunday was Pastor Anniversary Sunday, and the 11:00 a.m. worship service was definitely a great service. One of the daughters preached that service. Her sermon was on prayer, and it was so powerful. I constantly go back multiple times throughout the year and listen to that message. It was a very understandable message on prayer. After she finished and the invitation to Christ was extended, the choir sang the Eddie James classic, "You've Been So Faithful." I was singing on the choir for this service, and Lord knows I enjoyed this service.

On this Sunday, even though we were at the end of the service, I felt that God still had something else in store. During the closing prayer and benediction, I could hear the musicians start to play the Albertina Walker classic song, *"I Can Go to God in Prayer."* Now the message of this song is something that every believer can relate to, and you definitely won't be able to sit still during this song. After the closing prayer and benediction, musicians played louder and even though the service had ended, the Holy Spirit kept moving. The choir started singing, and I turned to the soprano section to see was the lady who ministers the song still there. She came down from the soprano section and started singing. Those in the congregation who were leaving ended up turning around and joining in the praise that was going on. The way the Holy Spirit was moving, I really was having a very hard time containing my praise. Yes, I always clapped my hands and shouted "Amen" in church, but I've also tried my best not to completely let loose. But now as an adult, I know that what the Holy Spirit wants, the Holy Spirit gets. Whether He's telling me something to do, convicting, leading me, even when it comes to praise and worship, I obey the Lord.

The song and the message were hitting me hard! When she started singing the part in the song that says, *"He Can Work It Out,"* that was it! All I can remember from that moment is feeling free and not caring about nothing or no one around me. This needed to happen because I've always held back in church; it was time for the Holy Spirit to have his way. Since that day, I have not held back. God deserves all of our praise, glory, and honor! I believe we all have been to a place where we worried too much about what people will say when we let loose in praise to God. This Sunday will always stand out in my mind because I learn so much more about praising God. It was always easy for me to praise and worship God at home, but I always held back at church. This was no longer an issue; I felt free.

Everything has been different since then; I do not mind praising God any and everywhere. That song, *"I Can Go to God in Prayer,"* will forever hold a special place in my heart because the message is so powerful, and plus, it will always remind me of when I truly opened up with praise to God in church. The year 2010 was a great year. I began to have a sense the Lord telling and showing me that He was preparing me to move me to another church.

CHAPTER 20

LIFE IS CHANGING

(2011)

BY THE TIME 2011 ARRIVED, I knew for a fact my time at Mt. Calvary was coming to an end. I will go more into this in Chapter 22, but I must point out a few things. This chapter is going to be short but straight to the point. My life was changing so much, and I started to see why God was moving me. Honestly, I really did not want to accept it. I loved (and still do love) Mt. Calvary, and the thought of me joining another church terrified me.

Slowly, I started to see that the situation I was in was like a child who needed to leave home. I had grown up at Calvary and learned so much. Now it was time for me to move out and go be an adult. That's the kind of situation it was. I had gotten too comfortable at Mt. Calvary, and it's not good to be too comfortable. The tools and lessons that had been planted into me have helped me a lot over the years. I was getting older.

I had a calling to preach. I couldn't run away from that calling any longer. The ministry that I started in 2002 was growing. Plus, God told me to trust Him. I knew that going into 2011 was most likely going to be my last full year as an official member of Mt. Calvary. I say official because it's been over a decade since I left, but I have never stopped considering myself a member of Mt. Calvary. I will never forget where I come from nor forget my love for Calvary.

By the time November 2011 arrived, it was time once again for Choir Day. Going into this particular Choir Day, I knew that this was going to be special and rememberable.

CHAPTER 21

CHOIR DAY

(2011)

I THOUGHT CHOIR DAY 2011 was going to be the last time I ever sang with the choir at Mt. Calvary, but it wasn't. I'll talk more about that in Chapter 24. It's a true example of never say never. Choir Day 2011 was overall a great time in the Lord. The ending of the program was the part that really blessed me. The last three songs that were ministered were *"It's About Time for A Miracle," "It Won't Be This Way Always,"* and a combined selection with all choirs of Mt. Calvary, *"God Made Me."* I broke down in tears during *"It Won't Be This Way Always"* because I knew this was most likely the last Choir Day I will ever participate in with Mt. Calvary.

I knew that 2012 was going to most likely be the year God moves me to where He wanted me. By that time, I pretty much knew where God wanted me to go. Also, by this time, I had been notified that I was being offered an opportunity to have my ministry on an Internet Radio Network starting in January

2012. This year was shaping up to be a very interesting year for me. God was opening up so many doors, but this particular Choir Day was the hardest to get through. At this point, only one person knew I was going to leave. Of course, that changed as time went on.

Choir Day at Mt. Calvary was and still is one of the most exciting programs that I look forward to every year. Even going back to when each choir used to have its own anniversary concert, I've always loved Mt. Calvary's choir anniversary programs. I'm just glad to know that Choir Day 2011 was not the last time I sang with the combined choirs for Choir Day.

Finally, I had to make a very hard decision. I had to choose whether to ignore what God was telling me to do and stay at Mt. Calvary or go to where He wanted me. By the time February 2012 arrived, I had made that very hard decision.

ONE OF THE HARDEST DECISION I HAD TO MAKE

I DID NOT WANT TO LEAVE MT. CALVARY, but I knew God was telling me to do so. I knew there were going to be people who either didn't understand or would make random assumptions about me leaving. I made the decision to do what God wanted. I had told the people that I wanted to know and people who needed to know that I was leaving.

There is something you must understand. I was twenty years old when I made this decision. Even though I knew God would never put me in harm's way nor set me up to fail, I still had a childlike mind at this point in my life. I still didn't want to do what God wanted because I did not want to leave a church that I loved and was comfortable attending. Some of you may say I was wrong for not wanting to do what God instructed me to do but, all of us have moments in which we wrestle with obeying the leading of the Lord. Even after I decided to go, I still could not picture myself actually being a member of a church that was not Mt. Calvary. I did not tell more people I was leaving because it would have been easy for someone to convince me to stay. Looking back, I'm glad I listened to God and joined the church He told me to join.

Frankly, it didn't make sense until late 2012 how important my decision to leave Mt. Calvary was. As I mentioned in a previous chapter, leaving Mt. Calvary was like a child leaving home to learn how to make it on their own. Leaving Mt. Calvary and joining another church was a huge step in my walk with Christ. What I learned at Mt. Calvary helped me to learn and grow at the church I joined. It also helped me to mature in life and in the Word of God. I posted a status on Facebook the day before writing this chapter, which read *"When God tells you to do something . . . do it!"* It may sound easier said than done, but it's an absolute must.

The way I left Calvary was kind of unexpected. I was going to finish out February 2012 and join my new church the first Sunday in March. However, when I visited my new church on the second Sunday in February, during the invitation to Christ, the Lord spoke to me and said, "Go join." Now I actually had the nerve to try to argue with the Lord. In my mind, I was telling Him, "No, that's not in order. This is not how I wanted to leave Mt. Calvary and join here." Then the Lord said again, "Go join." I realized I wasn't going to win this argument, and looking back on it, I was foolish to tell the Lord what I wanted to do and ignore what He was telling me to do. I took a deep breath and walked the aisle.

Everyone clapped as I walked to the front of the church to sit on the front pew. I was so excited and happy. I felt God's presence with me, but deep down I was hurting because I was joining another church. I wanted to cry, but I held it together and smiled. I knew I wasn't going to understand everything that God was doing in my life at that moment, but I knew it would make sense later on. I knew that in order for me to get use to my new church home, I had to focus on where I'm at. Other than one night of revival and slipping in at the end of some services on Sunday, I did not attend a full Mt. Calvary Sunday Service for five months. That was so hard, and (at that point) it was the longest I had gone without attending a service at Mt. Calvary.

I love the church God sent me to, and I'm glad I was obedient. Writing this chapter brought back that feeling of fear and uncertainty I had when I joined my new church home. As time went on, I've learned so much and have grown a lot in Christ. It made me even more grateful that I listened to God and thankful for the lessons I learned at Mt. Calvary.

I told my new pastor about my calling to preach. I was licensed to preach on Sunday, January 10, 2016 after preaching my initial sermon. I was ordained on Sunday, December 19, 2021. I have come far out of my comfort zone at my new church home and currently as of this writing, I'm the youth minister.

Most importantly, my relationship with Jesus Christ has grown tremendously! I'm very happy about all that God has done. The hard decisions didn't feel good nor made sense at first, but you've got to decide what's best. Nevertheless, this decision was hard to make, but it was definitely the right decision. After leaving, a lot of people didn't understand why I would leave Mt. Calvary since I didn't really want to leave. When God is speaking, it's not a voice you can easily ignore, especially when He's telling you to do something. I had to do what He wanted me to do. This hard decision was just another part in my growth and for that, I have no regrets. Mt. Calvary has always been in my heart since leaving. I will talk more about that in Chapter 27.

CHAPTER 23

THE USHER'S MINISTRY

I WAS A JUNIOR USHER at Mt. Calvary for ten years. Being an usher was more than just something I did every second and fourth Sunday. Honestly, I did not realize it until I was older how important an usher's job is. When someone enters the sanctuary, the first person they interact with is an usher. That interaction is so important because you never know what someone is going through. For years, I was always told about my smile when I was ushering. I didn't know what was so special about my smile, but it made a lot of people happy while entering the sanctuary. You never know what a smile and a simple welcome can do. I'm a third-generation usher; my grandparents, father, and I were ushers. Matter of fact, most of my dad's side of the family were ushers at one point.

My junior usher days were so much fun and rememberable. Of course, you already have read when I became an usher. But what I didn't mention is how even though I stopped ushering two years before leaving Mt. Calvary, I never stopped supporting the ushering ministry. I never missed an usher anniversary nor the Rainbow Tea (a fundraiser). When the junior usher ministry was put back together, there were three advisors of the junior usher ministry. Sadly, they all have gone on to be with the Lord now. They really loved what they did and were loved by everyone.

While writing this Chapter, Mt. Calvary just opened back to in person worship service for the first time since the COVID pandemic, in March 2020, a few weeks ago. Of course, the ushers at Mt. Calvary are still to this day, very welcoming. It's been well over a decade since I stopped ushering, but I still remember everything when it comes to ushering. The attire we wear and when the attire changes is still fresh on my mind. I know that the usher anniversary is every third Sunday in August and the Rainbow Tea is every Saturday before the second Sunday. I still even remember the usher hand signals. I loved the opportunity to make the hand signal for the ushers to have a seat after the pastor says his sermon subject. I remember the junior ushers having a car wash to raise money for our t-shirts that we wanted to wear on fourth Sundays. That car wash was fun and rememberable. I remember during my second or third year, we had free clothes give away. Now that was fun too. So many people in the community came to get free clothes. I absolutely loved that! The last thing I want to mention in this chapter is the usher march. One thing I was looking forward to when I started ushering was participating in the usher march. I absolutely loved marching; I write this with a smile on my face.

I started ushering in September 2000. I didn't march for

the first time until a few Sundays afterward. I remember ushering on the door one Sunday and being pulled out into the hallway by one of the senior ushers. I was asked to practice marching in place, and I asked, "Will I be marching soon?" She replied, "You will be marching today." That shocked me and made me nervous, but I was excited as well. The usher march always takes place during the offering when everyone walks around to put their offering in the offering basket. By the time the offering took place all of the ushers was lined up outside of the center doors. At that time, I was the only child ushering. This was before more kids joined. I lined up with the ushers, and we started getting our rhythm together. I wish I could remember what song the choir was singing that Sunday, but I do remember one of the sons of the house getting on the microphone announcing, "Ushers on The March." It was always the same son of the house who did that, and we knew it was time for us to move quickly so we wouldn't hold up the service. The center doors opened, and we started marching in. Most of the church was standing and clapping while the choir sang. Everybody was looking at me because I was the only child and I stood out. I passed my family while marching, and they was smiling at me. By the time we reached the door on the other aisle and marched out, I was so happy that it was over. After that, I really was not super nervous marching anymore.

During the usher's anniversaries every year, my nerves was always bad during the usher's march because the usher's union of Georgia was always there. That march was always hard for me because I didn't want to mess up. I always looked forward to it because the same song played for every usher march during the usher's anniversary.

"Tell Heaven (Tell Heaven)
Lord I'm coming (Lord I'm coming)
Lord I'm coming on home someday"

That's just a little snippet of the song; it never gets old. I'm sitting here at my desk and just happen to look over at my wall and notice some certificates I forgot about. I was *Junior Usher of the Month* and *Junior Usher of the Year* in 2002. I also was *Junior Chief Usher* a few times throughout the years. Honestly, what I truly gained mostly from my usher years was the importance of smiling and assisting others. Whether in church or in life, being an usher taught me a lot. I will never ever forget what I have gained from my ushering days at Mt. Calvary.

The Choirs and Music Ministry

Mt. calvary choirs hold a special place in my heart and always will. My pastor told me at one time that when the choir ministers on Sunday morning, its preparation for the preaching of God's Holy Word. This is true, but for me personally, it was so much more. My many memories of Sunday mornings and choir anniversaries floods my heart and mind right now. The many musicians that have passed through Mt. Calvary are a list of God-gifted musicians. I enjoyed my time there as a choir member and drummer.

The times that stick out for me is my younger years sitting in the pews watching them minister and learning more about Jesus through song. I can sit here and write about the many songs that the choir has sang over the years, but that would take up a lot of pages. With my pastor's sermons and the choirs singing, it made me hungrier for Jesus Christ. I wanted to know more about him. It also made me more curious. A funny story I want to tell is something I almost told in the last chapter, but I decided it was better to write it in this one. My favorite usher post was the choir stand, for many reasons. I talked about this in Chapter 7 a little bit, but I want to go into more detail. These are the three main reasons that I loved to user in the choir stand.

1) It was close to the pulpit; I loved being close to the pulpit. It enabled me to focus better on the sermons.
2) I was super close to the choir. I loved being close to the choir when they ministered through song.
3) I loved to stand in the midst of the musical instruments worshipping God (piano, drums, guitar, keyboard, and organ). At one time an organ was in the mix.

The message of every song is extremely important. But when you have a great tune to go with it, is just as important. It sounded so beautiful hearing the music that close. Two instruments I always have wanted to learn were the piano and organ. I used to sometimes peek and try to see whoever is playing. I would try to see how they played and would go back home to try it on my keyboard. It was hard to pick up tips from them because I didn't want them to think I was staring. I'm laughing so hard at that now because I used to be so determined to learn the piano and organ. I still am honestly. Hopefully, it will happen one day soon.

Something even funnier, I learned the drums from watching a drummer at Mt. Calvary. I got my first drum set in 1997.

It took me a few years, but I got the hang of playing the drums in 2003. As you can see, the choirs and music ministry has played a huge role in my life. A few chapters ago I mentioned that after I left Mt. Calvary in 2012, I thought I would never have a chance to sing with the choir at Mt. Calvary ever again. However, in 2019, former choir members were invited back to be a part of Choir Day. I'm so glad I was a part of that choir day program. It did feel surreal because I thought I would never have that opportunity again. It felt so good to minister with the choir at Mt. Calvary again. It definitely was needed in my life at the time because I was dealing with so much during that time period. Going back to Mt. Calvary's choir rehearsals was so exciting because as I have already mentioned in a previous chapter, Mt. Calvary's choir rehearsals didn't feel like choir rehearsals. When the Holy Spirit takes over, it turns into praise and worship instead of just rehearsing songs. Being back at Calvary and sitting in the tenor section again felt so good. Choir Day 2019 was an awesome time in the Lord!

Here is a funny fact: the choir I used to sang with at my new church home was on the program for Choir Day 2019 at Mt. Calvary. Soon as I was done singing with Mt. Calvary, I had to go sing with my new church family. One thing I can say about both of my church families: their choir and music ministry is incredible and anointed. By the time Choir Day 2019 was over, I was exhausted. My body was physically exhausted, but my heart and soul were leaping for joy!

There hasn't been a Choir Day since 2019 due to the COVID–19 pandemic. I can't wait for Mt. Calvary to have its first Choir Day celebration since 2019 in the near future.

Thank God for videos, DVDs, cassette tapes, and CDs; I'm continuously being ministered to. I love Mt. Calvary's Music Ministry and choirs so much; they will always hold a very special place in my heart.

CHAPTER 25

SUNDAY SCHOOL MEMORIES

I MAINLY ATTENDED BIBLE STUDY from ages five to thirteen. After thirteen, I attended off and on. My earliest Sunday school memories is being in the beginners Sunday school class. I remember the Easter (Resurrection) Sunday program in 1996. The funny part about this is during our skit, I was with a group of kids and they turned and faced everyone, but I didn't turn and face everyone. I stayed looking the other way because I was so nervous to face everyone. Another memory is having great Sunday school lessons, then going to the activity room with all the other classes to present what we learned in the lesson. We would sing a hymn, the classes would present, and the secretary would give the financial and attendance report from the previous Sunday. Then the church school superintendent would ask a child to do the prayer. I was able to do the prayer a few times, and I knew kids my age would always look forward to possibly being chosen to do the prayer. Then when it's your birthday, the Church School department would present a birthday card to whoever's birthday it was. I still have my cards in storage somewhere, I believe.

Speaking of the church school superintendent, she was a very nice lady! She went home to be with the Lord years ago. I will never forget her kindest and dedication as Church School superintendent. All my Sunday school teachers at Mt. Calvary have been so awesome. One fact that has always stood out from my time in the juniors' Sunday school class is that class got me started carrying a folder in church. I know it sounds silly, but I remember back then I used to carry so many papers and different things to church. One thing that taught us all is creating a folder to keep our belongings and Sunday school book all in one place so we won't lose anything. It also taught us about responsibly. Since then, I've always carried either a folder, journal, or a carry bag with me at church.

Organization is so important to me. I'm not perfect with it, though. I take it very seriously. Some of my Sunday school teachers have gone home to be with the Lord, and there are many that are still here. I will never forget the memories and lessons from Sunday school. My inner child really came out while writing this chapter.

CHAPTER 26

My Home Church Pastor

It's been a year since I started working on this book. Months after starting on this book, my home church pastor retired as pastor from Mt. Calvary. He still means a lot to me and will always mean a lot to me. I absolutely appreciate everything that he's done for me and the lessons I learned from him over the years. A poem he has quoted for years is a poem I keep taped in my Bible, along with the hymns, *I Must Tell Jesus, Blessed Assurance and Redeemed*. It's called, *God's Minute*, and it was written by the late Dr. Benjamin E. Mays.

I've only just a minute,
Only sixty seconds in it.
Forced upon me, can't refuse it,
Didn't seek it, didn't choose it,
But it's up to me to use it.

I must suffer if I lose it,
Give an account if I abuse it,
Just a tiny little minute,
But eternity is in it."

Over the years, I have learned so much about the importance of "God's Minute." There is no time to waste at all! I've learned that from him, and it's something I have applied to my life so much. I will always be very grateful for every lesson he has taught and for every time he encouraged me. A lot of people move on and forget what they've learned and who has inspired them. I am definitely one who doesn't forget, and honestly, I cannot forget. Especially being a preacher now, there's a lot he said in sermons or Bible study lessons that stand out in my life now. I know there are people my age or a little bit younger who will never forget the ABCs of life he gave us. He would have us recite it every Sunday after giving our tithes and offering. Along with that, we would have to recite John 3:16 and Proverbs 3:5–6.

"For God so loved the world, that he gave his only
begotten Son, that whosoever believeth in him
should not perish, but have everlasting life.
JOHN 3:16 (KJV)

"Trust in the LORD with all thine heart; and lean
not unto thine own understanding. In all thy ways
acknowledge him, and he shall direct thy paths.
PROVERBS 3:5–6 (KJV)

Then there was also a poem we would also have to recite called, *"Myself"* by Edgar Guest. I still carry it around in my Bible to this day. I didn't even realize how much I was applying the ABCs of life to life until I got older and noticed it while randomly reading them one day. I just said "applying." The A in the ABCs of life is Apply yourself. As I said earlier in this book, my pastor taught me about the importance of prayer. Prayer is something I truly believe in! The effectual fervent prayers of the righteous does avail much. Prayer is truly the key, and faith unlocks the door. All of these years after my childhood, *"I Must Tell Jesus"* is still not just my favorite hymn, it's always a go-to when I'm preparing to pray. No one can minister that hymn like my pastor. I can remember always making sure I spoke to him after church service when I was a kid, and I always wrote down something encouraging in a note and gave it to him. That memory just crossed my mind while writing this chapter.

There are more memories that I will never forget is how much he is led by the Holy Spirt. There have been times that the Holy Spirit is moving so much in service, he extended the invitation to Christ in the middle of the service. Another thing I remember is no matter who or where, if someone makes the decision to come to Christ, he will stop what he's doing and explain to that person the importance of that decision and pray with them, then everyone rejoices because of someone else getting saved. I'll never forget me and my family walking in one Sunday in the side door. We saw a crowd around his office. Come to find out someone had decided to come to Christ, and he helped that person right then and there. One Sunday when someone accepted Christ and was going to be baptized, he said something to my pastor. Baptism service was scheduled for that coming Tuesday night. He told my pastor that he had to leave the following day (he was in the army). My pastor got that look on his face, and everyone in church noticed it. He looked to one of the deacons and pointed at the baptism pool. Some of the deacons went up to the baptism pool and started running water into the pool. The young man and my pastor left the service to get ready for the baptismal. Shortly, one of the ministers told the pastor that the water would have to warm up and that baptism would be held later that evening instead. The fact that my pastor stopped everything he was doing to make sure that the young man was going to be baptized before going back to the army shows how Spirit-led he is.

Then one time he was in the middle of his sermon, and the power went out. He did not stop, he kept preaching. He has a voice that can be heard without a microphone, so he could still be heard (well, to me at least). The way he talks and how his voice fills a room, you can tell God has a special anointing on him. Another memory that stands out is the Sunday his mother passed. He found out in the middle of worship service. He stepped out momentarily but returned and didn't say anything. After the choir sang, he preached, and afterwards, extended the invitation to Christ, and gave the right hand of fellowship to the new church members and those who just got baptized. But right before he started communion, he told the congregation that his mother passed. We were all in shock. I was eleven at the time. I realized even then how much strength it took for him to preach God's Word after receiving the news about his mother. He told us that while he was planning to get one of his associate ministers to preach the service, he said he heard his mother's voice telling him to preach. Overall, I know it took the guidance and help of the Holy Spirit to give him the strength to preach after losing her.

At the end of the day, my pastor is definitely a man who is all about God's business. I cannot believe I almost forgot about this memory I'm about to share. During my junior usher days, I remember after Sunday school, we used to wait in the hallway until his office door opened and he called all the ushers, deacons, and ministers into his office for prayer. I used to be so excited for that. Of course, prayer was the main reason I was excited, but there was another reason. I used to look forward to going into his office. I always found his office fascinating. I'm smiling so hard right now because my mind is like a time machine right now. The first thing I always did when I first walked in his office was look at his robe closet which was open. I used to love to see his different robes for the past and present. Then after I did that, we all gathered in a huge circle in his office. He would always ask "Does anyone have a special prayer request?" Afterward, he would go into prayer. He sometimes would give us a few words of wisdom before he started praying, and I was all ears. I forgot to tell in the chapter about when I joined the Usher Ministry is that I didn't have to wait until my first Sunday of ushering to go into his office for prayer. That same Sunday, he told me to come into his office with the ministers, ushers, and deacons. Before he got started, he said, "Let us all welcome our newest usher." Everybody clapped, and I was kind of nervous because everyone was looking at me, but I was so excited at the same time. That was my first time going into his office for prayer.

I did not like missing prayer. I would be so mad at myself when I was late and missed prayer sometimes. There are so many great memories about him that I will never forget. He has now retired but has left behind an awesome legacy! His preaching, teaching, and singing has ministered to so many and has led so many to Jesus Christ. I could not finish writing this book and not mention this Man of God. I'm definitely sure he's going to read this, and I just want to personally thank him for all he has done for me and also for the community.

Something that I have always preached and taught in my ministry is "Only What You Do for Christ Will Last." I can definitely say one thing about my home church pastor, he has accomplished a lot. He is a great man.

CHAPTER 27

MT. CALVARY WILL ALWAYS BE HOME

I KNOW MY LIFE'S PURPOSE, and I know what God wants me to do. I have seen beautiful places, and I know I will be seeing more beautiful places. I have met a lot of great people, and I know I will meet even more great people. No matter where I go or who I meet, I will never forget Mt. Calvary Baptist Church. I'm so glad when I have the chance to visit Mt. Calvary. That church will always be home to me. I will forever carry the lessons and memories from Mt. Calvary with me. None of us are perfect nor have lived a perfect life. I want to encourage you to never forget who has helped you to become who you are today.

It's amazing how I have shared many memories and lessons, but more things keep coming to mind. I can remember on the Sundays we had more than one service. After service, most people would go to eat at local restaurants. Many times, I have walked into restaurants and saw a lot of people from church.

We always took the time from our meal to talk about worship service, the upcoming services, or just about life. Those used to be fun times; the fellowship was always fun.

I remember standing in the hallway after Sunday school, waiting on my mom or grandmother. I was super short, so everybody looked like a giant to me. I was constantly getting hugs and getting my cheeks pinched. I remember most of the deacons coming down the hallway, and each of them would come shake my hand. I remember that my neck sometimes was hurting because I was looking up. I loved greeting people, but sometimes looking up hurt my neck. It's very funny to me now looking back at that.

I always believe in passing down what I've learned to the next generation. I'll share about this man named Jesus Christ. I will preach about Him, teach about Him, and write about Him. I will always do what I need to do to tell the world about Jesus Christ. When someone asks me about where I met Jesus Christ, my mind will always go back to Mt. Calvary. That's where I met Jesus and that's where my relationship started with Him. Mt. Calvary will always hold a special place in my heart. As I bring this book to a close, my mind once again wonders back to another hymn that was ministered by my home church pastor during altar call. I'm always going to want to tell Jesus all of my trials because I truly cannot bear my burdens alone. But this hymn added even more assurance for me personally when it comes to loving, trusting, and having a relationship with Jesus Christ. The words to this hymn are:

"Blessed assurance, Jesus is mine
Oh, what a foretaste of glory divine

Heir of salvation, purchase of God
Born of His spirit, washed in His blood

This is my story, this is my song
Praising my Savior all the day long
This is my story, this is my song
Praising my Savior all the day long."

I thank God for the lessons and memories from Mt. Calvary Baptist Church!

BLESSED ASSURANCE

More Lessons & Memories from Calvary

~ PART II ~

COMING SOON!

Bertram Be'Jay Major

bejministries16@gmail.com

CHOICE PUBLISHING

P.O. Box 453
Powder Springs, Georgia 30127
www.entegritypublishing.com
info@entegritypublishing.com